HOW TO WRITE GOOD ENGLISH

C.W.E. Peckett

Published by
Thornhill Press
24 Moorend Road
Cheltenham.
MCMXC1

ISBN 0 946328 37 4

Typesetting by Wyvern Typesetters, Worcester.
Printed in Great Britain by
Billing & Sons Ltd, Worcester

How to Write Good English

Contents

Preface.

This book deals with Written, not Spoken English, for Spoken English has its own problems.

Why do we write? Surely we do so in order to convey a message to someone who cannot ask questions if he does not fully understand what we have written. Therefore we must write simply, clearly and accurately, so that there can be no misunderstanding. Moreover the reader cannot see or hear us; he cannot see the expression on our faces, or hear the tone of our voices, both of which we use to convey emphasis. Therefore we must find other ways of doing this. But if we write simply clearly and accurately, and give the right word the right emphasis, then we are writing good English.

But writing Good English is very difficult. There are two main reasons for this. One is that English has the largest vocabulary of all languages. This is because so many different peoples have lived in England, first the Celts, then the Romans, then the Danes and Anglo-Saxons, and then the Normans. All these have contributed to our vocabulary, and in addition, when scholars rediscovered Latin Literature during the Renaissance, they brought into existing English a very large number of words derived from Latin. Therefore there are often several words in English which have almost the same meaning, and it is difficult to choose the right one. One authority has defined Good Style as 'the right word in the right place.'

The other main reason is that there are so few rules for writing English. Writing Latin is comparatively easy because the language has so many rules. Once we have learned what they are, and if we keep to them, it is almost impossible to write bad Latin. But the writer of English is like a dog wandering off his lead in a road full of traffic: he may easily come to grief.

Therefore this book gives only simple rules for writing Good English. It deals with various examples of Bad English and shows how to avoid them. But the best way to learn how to write Good English is to read a large number of books written by authors who are acknowledged to be good writers, and then to imitate their style. Perhaps this book will help to show why it is good.

The answers to the Exercises have not been given. Pupils therefore cannot be tempted to look them up, and so can gain the full benefit of using their brains.

Section 1. About the Verb

A verb is a word which describes an action. It is the most important word in the sentence. Indeed it is possible to write a sentence which has only the verb in it.

e.g. *'Go.' or 'Help.' or 'Wait.'*

But these are only commands and we do not know who is performing the action of the verb. Normally the sentence is only complete when it tells not only about the action but who performs it. This can be done by using 'I', 'you', 'he', 'she' or 'it', 'we' or 'they'.

e.g. *He goes. I help. They waited.*

Often it is a person or thing which performs the action.

e.g. *The man goes. The medicine helps. The girls waited.*

We call the person or thing that performs the action the 'Subject'.

Very often a word is written in front of the verb to show whether it tells of a Past, Present or Future action.

These words are: 'have', 'has', 'was' or 'were' (Past)
'am', 'are' or 'is' (Present)
'shall' or 'will' (Future).

e.g.*He has gone.* or *They were going.* (Past)
I am helping. or *She is helping.* (Present)
We shall wait. or *You will wait.* (Future)

These words are really part of the verb and show whether what we call its 'Tense' is Past, Present or Future.

Therefore a complete sentence needs only three words in it, as above; but of course a sentence is often more complicated. In the following sentence:

The deer will eat all that grass.

'The deer' is the subject, 'will eat' is the verb, and its Tense is Future.

Exercise A From the following sentences pick out (1) the Subject, and (2) the verb; and (3) say what its Tense is.

1) They are walking along the path.
2) The monkeys have eaten all those nuts.
3) That balloon will fly over the forest.
4) I shall not see you again.
5) Why were you looking into that window?
6) The carpenter is having a rest.

7) The poor men work all day.
8) The dustmen have taken away all the rubbish.
9) When will you come to my house?
10) Many people are crowding into the stadium.

(*Note.* The word 'one' is sometimes used to show that the Subject is an unknown person,'someone' or 'anyone'.

e.g.*From this window one can see the forest.*

This is not Good English. Indeed it is almost French, for the word 'one' is being used as if it were derived from the French 'on' = 'a person'. In Good English we would write 'you',

i.e. From this window you can see the forest.

even though we were not addressing a definite person.)

Exercise B Complete the following sentences.

1) Yesterday the cattle   grazing in this field.
2) My friends, I hope   will not do that to me again.
3) The bookmaker is   the horses through field-glasses.
4) We   now trying hard.
5)   will all come home tomorrow.
6) He   speaking, but we paid no attention.
7) The cook is   the cake into the oven.
8) The cake   soon be baked.
9)   was making that noise?
10) I   never seen such a thing before.

A sentence must have a verb, otherwise it does not make sense. Take for instance Sentence 2 in Exercise A above. Suppose we wrote it without a verb as

The monkeys all those nuts.

It does not tell us what the monkeys have done, are doing or will do to the nuts. So it makes no sense. We can only guess its meaning. Perhaps the monkeys have hidden the nuts, or will steal them. How can we tell? Only by having the verb in the sentence.

Unfortunately some modern authors, especially those who write stories about crime or adventure, have taken to writing sentences without verbs.

e.g. *They hurried on. Further and further. Through the woods to the beach. There at last on the beach . . .the boat.*

The author has written like this to make things more exciting. He hopes that the reader will realise that 'they' are hurrying quicker and perhaps more anxiously.

But when we examine the passage we cannot be sure what it means. 'Further and further' is apparently a sentence because it ends with a full stop. But what does it mean? We can give the author the benifit of the doubt by deciding that 'They hurried on further and further.' But did they 'hurry' or 'run' or even 'gallop' through the woods? And what about the boat on the beach? It couldn't 'hurry'. Was it just there? Or did they see it?

The passage written in Good English might be:

They hurried on further and further. They hurried (or ran) through the woods to the beach, and there at last they saw the boat.

Exercise C Rewrite the following passages in Good English.

1) The engine was switched off. No sound from anywhere. No movement any more.
2) Seven o'clock in the morning. I looked through the window. Dark clouds in the sky. Rain perhaps? I did not care.
3) I opened the cupboard and looked inside. Bottle of water. Paper cups. Plastic bottle with a screw cap.
4) I lay on the bare mattress. Cold. Blanket I thought. A terrible effort to get up and find one.
5) A car drew up outside. Footsteps coming through the front door. Coming to the door of my room. Stopping there.

In Good English every sentence must have a Verb.

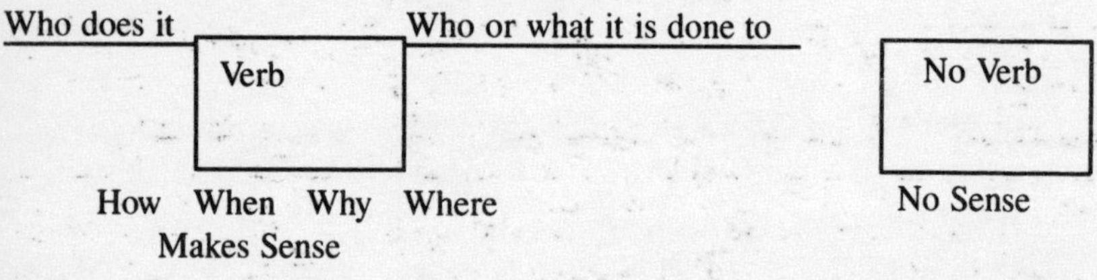

Section 2 The use of 'will' and 'shall'. Split Infinitive.

In section 1 we noted that we show that the verb is in the Future Tense by adding 'will' or 'shall' to it. We use 'shall' when the Subject is 'I' or 'we' and 'will' when the Subject is someone or something else.

e.g. **I shall** *go to town tomorrow.*
We shall *come here again.*

They will *find the going difficult.*
The boy will *take the dog for a walk.*
The fire will *soon burn brightly.*

Some people find it hard to decide when to use 'shall' and when to use 'will'. They should remember the word 'wish'.

W I SH
'We' and 'I' go with 'Shall'

They will then know that they must use 'will' only with 'you', 'he', 'she', 'it', 'they' or some other Subject.

Americans tend to get this wrong, and to use 'will' with all Subjects.

e.g. **I will** *go to town tomorrow.*
We will *come here again.*

This is Bad English, and we are beginning to borrow it from the Americans. This is a pity, because it stops us using 'will' and 'shall' to add extra meanings to Verbs in the Future Tense. We can do this by breaking the rule about these two words mentioned above, i.e. by using 'will' when the Subject is 'I' or 'we' and by using 'shall' when the Subject is someone or something else.

Thus, if someone writes

I will go to town tomorrow.

he is not only foretelling what is going to happen; he is also showing that his feelings are involved, as if he said

I want to go to town tomorrow and so I shall do so.

Similarly, if a boy's mother says

Jimmy, will you stop that noise?

and he answers

No **I won't (will not).**

Jimmy is not merely foretelling what he will not do, but he is being rude as well. And if we write

That man shall pay us what he owes.

we are not merely foretelling that he will pay us; we are also implying that there will be trouble if he does not.

By using 'will' and 'shall' in this way we are adding emphasis to the Verb in the Future Tense, so we will call this use the Emphatic Future.

Perhaps this use of 'will' and 'shall' is a survival from the 16th century, when English was a more forceful language than it is now. In the Book of Common Prayer (1559) we find as the First Commandment:

I am the Lord, thy God: **thou shalt (you shall)** have none other gods but me.

where 'thou shalt' has the force of a command.
In Psalm 23 we find
The Lord is my shepherd . . .**he shall** feed me in a green pasture.
and in Psalm 25
Unto thee, O Lord, **will I** lift up my soul.

Exercise A Which of the following sentences has a Verb in the Future, and which one in the Emphatic Future?

1) I shall leave that to you.
2) We will save a lot of money.
3) You shall never see me again.
4) He will learn the hard way.
5) The enemy shall not conquer us.
6) The lights will be put out at 10p.m.
7) They are not willing to come here.
8) She will regret it.
9) I will find out where that noise is coming from.
10) Those foxes shall not kill my lambs.

Exercise B In the following sentences turn the Future into the Emphatic Future, and the Emphatic Future into the Future.

1) We shall be angry, if you do that.
2) No one shall cross this path.
3) I will not obey you.
4) These animals shall not leave their cage.
5) You will see me tomorrow.
6) The batsman will not hit this ball.
7) You shall have all you want.
8) The aeroplane will not fly over the city.
9) We will take that away from you.
10) I shall always respect such a man.

The Verb often has the word 'to' in front of it.

e.g. *to finish, to read, to write*

We call this use of the Verb the Infinitive. The word 'to ' is really part of the Infinitive and must not be separated from the Verb. Some people, however, do so, especially when speaking.

e.g. *to soon finish, to carelessly read, to carefully write*

It is wrong to allow this fault of spoken English to creep into written English.

If we write Good English, we never split an Infinitive.

Exercise C Correct the following sentences.

1) I hope to soon retire.
2) The dogs began to hungrily eat.
3) The girl likes to always sleep in this bed.
4) We shall try to never write bad English.
5) You wanted to kindly treat him.

Exercise D Improve the following.

1) They rushed outside. Crowds everywhere. Shouting. What was the matter?
2) We shall not do that. (Emphatic Future)
3) The police tried to quickly catch the thief.
4) The thief shall not get away. (Ordinary Future)
5) The waiters shall soon bring us the next course. (Ordinary Future)
6) The men were able to easily finish the job.
7) I shall certainly not wait for a whole week. (Emphatic Future)
8) He lay in the bed. Nearly asleep. A scuttling noise. A mouse perhaps.
9) You shall learn how to carefully search a house. (Ordinary Future)
10) This boy will be taught to never play such tricks.

Section 3 Use the Active instead of the Passive Verb

In English there are two kinds of Verbs, 'Active' and 'Passive'. The Active Verb describes an action which somebody or something does.

e.g. *John* **eats** *a biscuit.*
The horse **kicked** *the boy.*
The rain **will soften** *the soil.*

The Passive Verb describes an action which is done to somebody or something.

e.g. *A biscuit* **is being eaten** *by John.*
The boy **was kicked** *by the horse.*
The soil **will be softened** *by the rain.*

If the Verb is Passive, the word 'by' almost always comes in front of the person or living thing that performs the action.

e.g. *The cart is being pulled* **by** *the horse.*
We shall be bitten **by** *mosquitoes.*
This earth has been hoed **by** *the gardener.*

Exercise A Which of the following sentences has a Passive Verb?

1) We shall kill the enemy.
2) The enemy will be killed by us.
3) The scones were baked by the cook.
4) Who told that story?
5) Can that window have been broken by a man with a stone?
6) We can see it clearly.
7) I will put a net over the cabbages so that they will not be eaten by birds.
8) The girl is being photographed by her friends.
9) Where did you find that book?
10) This was written by me.

The Active Verb tells us what happened in fewer words and often more vividly than the Passive Verb does. If we read

The boy's leg was bitten by the dog.

we don't care very much. But if we read

The dog bit the boy's leg.

we can almost feel the pain.

Therefore use the Active Verb instead of the Passive whenever you can. In other words 'Make the person do the thing'.

Exercise B Improve the following sentences by using an Active Verb in place of the Passive one.

1) Will my work be corrected by the teacher?
2) Has this sentence been seen by her?
3) You are being cheated by that rogue.
4) The miracle was seen by a large crowd with their own eyes.
5) Why has this medicine not been drunk by the patient?
6) By whom was this book written?
7) I am afraid that we shall be killed by those soldiers.
8) That man's hair has been cut by a bad barber.
9) They are being arrested by the police.
10) The girls will not be terrified by those boys.

In some sentences that have a Passive Verb the thing that performs the action has in front of it not 'by' but 'with'.

e.g. *The fields are covered* **with** *snow.*

This is perfectly good English; but the verb can be made Active;

Snow covers the fields.

This emphasises 'snow', and perhaps means that there is a lot of it.

Similarly

Her eyes were filled with tears.

is good English, but it can become

Tears filled her eyes.

emphasising 'tears'.

But in other apparently similar sentences the verb cannot be made Active so easily.

e.g. *This soup has been flavoured with garlic.*

really means

This soup has been flavoured by someone (the cook?) with garlic.

So the version with the Active Verb would be:

Someone has flavoured this soup with garlic.

and it would give no special emphasis.

Garlic has flavoured this soup.

would be bad English.

Similarly

The gear-box has been lubricated with oil.

= The gear-box has been lubricated by someone with oil.
or Someone has lubricated the gear-box with oil.
and Oil has lubricated the gear-box.

would be strange English.

Use the Active Verb whenever possible: it is stronger than the Passive.

Exercise C Rewrite the following sentences in Good English.

1) The picture was admired by everyone.
2) Cars. Lorries. Motor bicycles. All tearing along the road. It was very dangerous.
3) We shall not be captured by the enemy. (Emphatic)
4) I will read that book this evening. (Unemphatic)
5) They asked all the people to slowly walk throught the cemetery.
6) It is better to regularly settle your debts.
7) These roses shall bloom for a long time. (Unemphatic)
8) This floor must be washed with a mop.
9) I shall eat a lot. (Emphatic)
10) The piano is being played by a good musician.

Section 4 Emphasis

We have seen in Section 1 that the Verb is the most important word in a sentence. No sentence can make sense without one. The next most important word in a sentence is the Subject; except in a command a sentence is useless if it does not tell us who performs the action.

To show how important the Subject is we put it as near as we can to the beginning of the sentence.

e.g. **The man** *had never seen such beautiful flowers.*

We can emphasise other words in the sentence by putting them near the beginning.

e.g. **Never** *had the man seen such beautiful flowers.*

Winston Churchill emphasised 'never' in this way during the last war in a speech about the few hundred fighter-pilots who stopped the German bombers devastating Southern England; '*Never* in the field of human endeavour has so much been owed by so many to so few.' If we emphasise 'never' like this, we can avoid the ugly way of doing so that is creeping into our language.

e.g. *I have never ever eaten such bad food.*

If we wanted to emphasise how beautiful the flowers were, we might write

Such beautiful flowers had the man never seen.

but that might be too poetic.

There is another device which we can use in written English to emphasise words. If the sentence

John saw a fox in the garden.

were spoken, the speaker would show by the tone of his voice the word that he wanted to emphasise. If he wanted to say

John (and nobody else) saw the fox in the garden.

he might say 'John' louder than the other words. If he wanted to show how amazed he was about the fox being in the garden, he would show this by the way he spoke.

In written English we cannot express such things by the tone of our voices. Instead we add 'It' and a suitable part of the verb 'to be' to the word we want to emphasise.

e.g. If we want to emphasise 'John', we write

It was John.

We then join this phrase to the rest of the sentence by the right form of 'who'.

It was John who saw a fox in the garden.

or I hit John with a stick.

becomes It was John whom I hit with a stick.

or John had a big nose.

becomes It was John whose nose was big.

But if the word we want to emphasise in this way is not a person, then we join the phrase to the rest of the sentence by 'that'.

e.g. In the sentence

John saw a fox in the garden.

if we want to express how amazed we are about the fox, we could write

It was a fox **that** John saw in the garden.

Or if we were surprised that such an animal as a fox could be in the garden, we would write

It was in the garden **that** John saw a fox.

If the tense of the verb is Present, we use 'It is'

e.g. *It is John who is winning the race.*

And if the tense of the verb is Future, use 'It will be'

e.g.*It will be John who wins the race.*

Note that, since the Future is shown by 'will be', 'wins' remains in the Present.

Going back to the sentence

The man had never seen such beautiful flowers.

we certainly cannot write

It was never that the man had seen such beautiful flowers

Nor can we emphasise 'always', 'sometimes' and other words indicating time in such a way. This is because such words are almost part of the verb, and we show that this is so by putting them between the two words 'had' and 'seen' which make up the verb.

i.e. had never seen

But other words indicating time, such as 'yesterday', 'to-morrow', 'next month' etc. can be emphasised by the above device.

e.g. *They told me yesterday.*

can be It was only yesterday that they told me.

and We shall not get a reply till next month.

can be It will be next month before we get a reply.

We can do this because such words are not so closely joined to the verb.

Exercise A Rewrite the following sentences emphasising the words in bold type.

1) We saw the kangaroo **yesterday**.
2) **That medicine** cured me.

3) The floods covered **only the low-lying fields.**
4) You will **not** find a better house **anywhere.**
5) **The foul air** caused my headache.
6) **The sailors** are making all that noise.
7) We can smell **garlic.**
8) They found the pigs **in the orchard.**
9) **The horses** were killed.
10) I like to drink wine **sometimes**.

Exercise B Rewrite the following in Good English.

1) I will ask her to thoroughly wash my clothes.
2) That will certainly never be done again by me. (Active Verb and Emphatic Future).
3) I find only writing difficult. (Emphasise 'only writing')
4) He looked into the bedroom. Drawers open. Dirty footmarks on the carpet, Who had done it? A thief?
5) We will usually be here on Sundays. (Unemphatic)
6) The police managed to just catch sight of the criminal.
7) A picture more beautiful than that has been painted by no one.
8) We shall do that because we want to. (Emphatic)
9) They liked walking best. (Emphasise 'walking')
10) They give hay only to cows. (Emphasise 'only to cows')

Section 5 Choosing the right word.

Perhaps the most difficult thing we find about writing Good English is choosing the right word to express simply, clearly and correctly the meaning that we want to convey. This is because there are so many words to choose from. English has the largest vocabulary of all languages, since so many people, Celts, Romans, Greeks, Danes, Anglo-Saxons and Normans, have contributed to it.

The Celts were in Britain by the end of the Bronze Age, and lived there almost undisturbed until the Romans conquered the country during the first century AD. The Celts seem to have adopted readily the language which the Romans spoke, perhaps because they brought with them a way of life which was better than that of the Celts. Consequently only a few Celtic words survive in the English Language, most of them names of places or rivers. But the Romans never penetrated into Wales, and so Celtic is still spoken in some places there.

During the 350 years while the Romans occupied Britain the inhabitants probably developed a British-Latin dialect which Julius Caesar might have found hard to understand. And if things had gone differently we might now be speaking a language rather like French. But in 407AD Roman legions who had defended Britain for so long, were withdrawn to protect other parts of the Roman Empire. Barbarians from Scandinavia at once began making raids on Britain, and by 450 the Jutes had settled in Kent. They were followed by Angles and Saxons who continued to invade and settle in the country for the next 150 years, so that they turned Britain into England. They were followed by the Danes.

These barbarians had no use for Roman-British civilisation. They imposed on the Roman-Britons not only their own way of life but also their own language. This Anglo-Saxon language was as robust as the people who spoke it, and it expressed simply and clearly, usually in words of one syllable, all that they wanted to say. But what they needed to say was not complicated.

They had to borrow some Romano-British words, for they found in Britain things that had not existed in their own country. For instance, in Scandinavia they lived either in widely separated huts, or in a few of them built together in an enclosure which they called a 'town'. They had never seen anything like the Roman cities which they found in Britain. It was typical of them that they borrowed not the Romano-British word for 'city', but the one for the military camp on which it was based, i.e. *castra,* which they pronounced as 'Chester'.

Similarly they found for the first time in these cities paved roads which the Romano-British called *strata.* So they borrowed the word and called them 'streets'.

In 596 Christianity was introduced into England and brought to the Anglo-Saxons many things and ideas which they had no words to express. The language of the Church was Latin, and so they had to adopt new words from the language, e.g. 'Pope', 'priest', 'monk', 'sacred' etc.

By the time of Alfred the Great (849-901) the Anglo-Saxons had become civilised and developed a language to express their civilised ideas. But it was still vigorous and simple and many of its words had only one syllable. Alfred translated into his own language a history book written in Latin. If we look at a paragraph taken at random from it, we find that it has 104 words, of which only 23 have more than one syllable, and 9 of them i.e. 'decoy', 'precious', 'catch', 'chief', 'tribute', 'consist', 'according', 'measure', 'tunic', were derived at some time from Latin.

In 1066 the Normans invaded England bringing with them their own dialect of Old French. The Norman knights were conquerors and did not mix with the conquered, so that for many years their language had little influence on Anglo-Saxon. But as trade grew, especially in London, the merchants formed a middle class, which helped to introduce many useful Norman words into Anglo-Saxon. By the late 14th century the Anglo-Norman language was large enough to convey adequately the thoughts of as great a writer as Chaucer, and in 1611 it was an almost perfect instrument for producing the Authorised Version of the Bible.

When the Renaissance reached England scholars brought into the English language thousands of words derived from Latin and Greek. They had to do this for some things like 'democracy' for which there was no word in English because it did not exisit in England. Other Greek and Latin words they anglicised because they expressed a slightly different shade of meaning from that conveyed by the corresponding Anglo-Norman word. But very often they introduced the new words to show how fascinated they were with this rediscovered literature. Such words were written rather than spoken.

Mathematicians, scientists, doctors and other specialists began, especially from the early 19th century onwards, to make up words mainly derived from Ancient Greek to express their new ideas and as names for their new apparatus and techniques.

We learn from this brief history of the English Language why its vocabulary is so large. We learn also that the Anglo-Saxon part of it, helped by some Norman words, served for about 1,000 years to express the thoughts of Englishmen simply, clearly and correctly.

It would be wrong, however, to lay down a rule that words derived from Anglo-Saxon should always be preferred to those derived from Latin or Greek. The latter can sometimes express a different shade of meaning. For instance 'think' is an Anglo-Saxon word, and 'conclude' is derived from Latin. Both show that the mind is working, but if we say

> I thought the man mad.

we mean

> The idea came into my head that the man was mad.

But if we say

> I concluded that the man was mad.

we mean

> I thought hard, and finally made up my mind that the man was mad.

Even some words derived from Anglo-French are better avoided when we have an Anglo-Saxon word which means the same. Thus it is better to use the Anglo-Saxon word 'begin' instead of the rather pompous Norman word 'commence'.

We might well recommend writers to study the Anglo-Saxon word first, and to decide whether it conveys adequately what they want to express, before using a word derived from Latin, Greek or French.

Exercise A Substitute in each sentence one of the following simple words for the one printed in bold type.

calm, cart, try, help, come, hide, letter, tale, near, noble, begin.

1) The young man came of an **illustrious** family.
2) The **vehicle** was so overloaded that the horse could not pull it.
3) The nurse **assisted** him in every way.
4) The **narrative** which he commenced to tell, was too difficult for me to understand.
5) There was a large house **in the vicinity of** the park.
6) He could not **conceal** the gun from the police.
7) They **attempted** to run away.
8) The tourists **arrived** too late to catch the train.
9) The **missive** that he sent me was full of mistakes.
10) You must **pacify** him before I can talk to him.

Exercise B Improve the following sentences by substituting a simple word for a more complicated one in each.

1) He did not observe what I was doing.
2) They suspended the basket from a branch of the tree.
3) Tell us what that signifies.
4) She was so obdurate that nothing would make her give way.
5) He was seized by a paroxysm of laughter.
6) The bird's plumage was all white.
7) The train arrived on schedule.
8) He responded in a loud voice.
9) The match was played annually.
10) The king and his consort were welcomed by the mayor.

Exercise C Rewrite the following sentences in Good English.

1) He refused to give his consent.
2) The police began to thoroughly question him.
3) The patient was well looked after by the nurses.
4) Tomorrow I will discover where he lives.
5) My coat was stolen by that man, I am sure.
6) We will receive a letter from him next week.
7) They worked so hard that they were covered with perspiration.
8) The fresh air invigorated us.

9) I hope to eventually win a prize.
10) The little pigs were being suckled by the sow.

Section 6 Avoiding the wrong word.

A noun is a word which we use to name anything. We call some nouns 'concrete' and others 'abstract'. A concrete noun gives the name of things, animals or people; an abstract noun gives the name of ideas. Thus 'grease' is a concrete noun, but 'greasiness' an abstract one. It is abstract nouns which cause most trouble when we try to write Good English.

Almost ninety years ago the poet John Masefield, who had been a sailor, wrote a poem which begins:

> I must go down to the sea again, to the lonely sea and the sky,
> and all I ask is a tall ship and a star to steer her by.'

Not a single word in these two lines is derived from Latin or Greek, and all the nouns are concrete. Therefore the lines tell us simply and forcefully how much he longs to go to sea again.

A writer of Bad English, so bad that it could never be published, might have written:

> 'I am filled with a great urgency to descend to the ocean again, to the lonely ocean and the celestial region, and I have one sole thing to ask for and that is a vessel with masts of considerable altitude, and a stellar object by which to navigate it.'

The abstract noun 'urgency' and the passive verb 'I am filled' take the force out of his longing.

'descend', derived from Latin, can be useful, but it usually describes a stately way of going down

e.g. *The mayor in his robes descended the stairs.*

'Ocean', 'celestial region' and 'stellar object', all derived from Latin, are too pompous.

'Sole' is derived from Latin and means 'one and only'. Since we already have 'one' the word 'sole' is superfluous.

'Navigate', derived from Latin, means not only 'steer' but 'perform all that is necessary to keep the ship on course.' It is a good word in the wrong place.

By far the worst phrase is 'masts of considerable altitude.' It is certainly not a clear and simple way of describing what old seamen call a 'tall ship', a magnificent three-masted one with square sails rigged one above the other on the lofty masts.

It is the abstract nouns 'urgency' and 'altitude' which produce the worst English in the above passage. In writing Good English we should avoid abstract nouns as much as possible, especially those ending in '-tion'. Scholars derived many of these from Latin, sometimes to express a new idea, but more often to show off their learning, or because they did not take enough trouble to express clearly what they wanted to say.

There are two ways of avoiding abstract nouns. One is to turn them into the corresponding verb.

e.g. *He had changed beyond* **recognition**.

is better written as

He had changed so much that no one **recognised** him.

And *I don't understand the* **implication** *of those words*

is better written as

I don't understand what those words **imply**.

Also *That sentence needs* **simplification** *by you.*

is better written as

You should **simplify** *that sentence.*

Another way of showing the abstract noun is to turn it into the corresponding adjective.

e.g. *This gives* **satisfaction.**

is better written as

This is **satisfying.**

And *He had many* **qualifications.**

is better written as

He was **qualified** *in many ways.*

Also *They were not moved by* **consolation.**

is better written as

They were **inconsolable.**

Politicians often use abstract nouns. Sometimes they do so just to be pompous. A minister who is asked in Parliament if something is true will often reply

The answer is in the negative.

Sir Winston Churchill, in his early days in Parliament, once said in order to make fun of an opponent's speech:

It cannot in the opinion of His Majesty's Government be classified as slavery in the extreme acceptance of the word without some risk of terminological inexactitude.

According to a newspaper report a recently elected politician said to his supporters:

> I hope I shall be able to live up to the expectations which you have put in my hands.

How did his supporters manage to get hold of such intangible things as 'expectations', and if they did so and put them into his hands, would they not have slipped through his fingers? What he meant was

> I hope I shall be able to do what you expected me to do when you voted for me.

Journalists use abstract nouns more often than other people. Several years ago journalists who wrote for less reputable papers were called 'tuppence-a-liners', because they were paid twopence for each line of print in the articles which they wrote. So it paid them to use as many long and complicated words as possible, and they came to use a language which we call 'Journalese'. A journalist who writes regularly for The Times says in one of his articles: 'Journalese as a separate register of English flourishes, with words and usages that nobody outside the inky trade would dream of using, even in a nightmare. We use this private language for various reasons: to save space in headlines, or merely as corroborative jargon, intended to give artistic verisimilitude to an otherwise bald and unconvincing narrative. Our journalese is designed to make our pieces about what is not worth knowing sound more important than they are. . .

When reading newspapers, you should remember that you are reading a different language.'

This Journalese is sometimes so obscure that it has to be translated into Good English. The following sentence was recently printed in a famous newspaper.

> Sustaining a sense of civic virtue is difficult now that society is seen purely as instrumental to individual gratification.

This, when translated, becomes

> It is difficult now for citizens to remain honest with one another, when they have come to think that by living together they can get what they please.

More examples of Journalese for comment and improvement are given in Section 10.

Exercise A Improve the following sentences by getting rid of the bold type abstract noun.

1) Several people made **applications** for this post.
2) He was filled with **exultation**.
3) They could not bear the **suspicion** of their neighbours.

4) The king wasted much time in **negotiations** with the enemy.
5) The nurse's work is worthy of our **commendation**.
6) We shall give the matter further **consideration**.
7) **Desperation** made him behave like that.
8) His **patriotism** caused him to face the enemy alone.
9) You have no **justification** for punishing him like that.
10) I am not in **agreement** with you.

Exercise B Improve the following sentences by getting rid of the abstract nouns.

1) They were full of amazement.
2) It is not our intention to make any improvement to this road.
3) They said the book was a funny one, but it did not afford me any amusement.
4) Your work deserves commendation.
5) The young man hid to escape conscription into the armed forces.
6) I am of the opinion that your knowledge of this is greater than mine.
7) The shopkeeper was under no obligation to return the money.
8) They have no recollection of what took place.
9) He speaks with great eloquence.
10) What you have written requires elucidation.

Exercise C Rewrite the following in Good English.

1) It was the rush hour. People everywhere. Platform crowded. The train! No possibility of getting to the door. I missed it.
2) I should like to really find out what happened.
3) Nobody observed what was going on.
4) The doctors had no anticipation of finding any treatment that would cause the patient's recovery.
5) They were amused not by the play but really by the actors.
6) We will never know why they made an alteration to their plans.
7) No recognition was given by anyone to her success.
8) I would like you to thoroughly overhaul my vehicle.
9) A demonstration was given us by the manager of how the computer should be utilised to provide a solution to this problem.
10) His desperation overcame his patriotism.

Section 7 Other words to avoid.

When we try to write Good English there are some words which we should use carefully or not at all. People who write Journalese or what we might call 'Jargon' often use words so carelessly that they lose their real meaning, or even mean nothing at all. In writing Good English it is often best to avoid such words and express our thoughts more simply and carefully in a different way.

Here is a list of words to avoid.

case

This word means either 'box', e.g. 'a case of wine', or 'law-suit', e.g. 'the defendant in a case of murder', or 'the occurrence of disease', e.g. 'There are many cases of typhoid.' But it is often used to convey none of these meanings; often indeed without any meaning at all.

A famous author, in a book about the First World War, wrote:'

In some cases balloons were used as decoys.

Balloons can have nothing to do with law-suits or doctors, so apparently they must have been put in boxes. If so, how did they fly? What the author really meant was

Often balloons were used as decoys.

In bad English the word 'case' is often used with no meaning at all, and can be left out.

e.g. *There are many cases of children who have lost their parents.*

is better written

There are many children who have lost their parents.

And *The books were in many cases badly printed.*

is better written

Many of the books were badly printed.

But '*in case'* can be a useful phrase.

e.g. *We had better take some pills in case we are seasick.*

Here 'in case', replaces the archaic 'lest' or the clumsy 'for fear that'.

instance

This word is used without meaning in exactly the same way as 'case'.

e.g. *There are many instances of children who have lost their parents.*

Several words are used badly because the writer wants to be pompous, and is not content with calling a spade a spade. He uses more words than necessary to express his meaning, and some of them can be left out. Such words are:

character

e.g. *The accident was caused by the dangerous character of the road.*

is better written

The accident was caused because the road was dangerous.

nature

e.g. *His actions were of a patriotic nature.*

is better written

His actions were patriotic.

condition

e.g. *He was carried home in an intoxicated condition.*

is better written

He was carried home intoxicated (or better still 'drunk').

quality

e.g. *My typing is of a better quality than yours.*

is better written

My typing is better than yours.

degree

e.g. *This painter's works show a high degree of skill.*

is better written

This painter's works show that he is very skilful.

issue

This is a difficult word to use since it has several meanings, i.e. 'something which is sent or comes out'; 'children'; 'the putting into circulation of banknotes, papers, books etc.'; 'a result'; 'the subject of a discussion in whose result we are interested'. In Parliament a MP might say

In his speech the Minister did touch upon this issue.

Since he did not touch upon children or the daily paper, this must mean

The Minister did not mention the subject we are arguing about.

Sometimes, however, 'issue' is used carelessly to mean nothing more than 'subject' or 'topic'.

e.g. *This issue is of great interest to farmers.*

In this sentence 'subject' would make better sense than 'issue'. An even better sentence would be

This is something which interests farmers.

such

This word can be very badly used.

e.g. *It is said that the man is a rogue; but such is not the case.*

instead of

It is said that the man is a rogue; but that is not true.

if

This word is used, of course, as a simple way of saying 'provided that' in a conditional sentence.

e.g. *If (provided that) you pay in advance, you will be given a discount.*

But some authors, even those who write in a good style, sometimes use this word wrongly, especially when they want to be too clever.

e.g. *The girl's face was beautiful, if a little pale.*

really means

If the girl's face was a little pale, it was beautiful.

The author should have written

The girl's face was beautiful, **though** *a little pale.*

hopefully

Americans use this word wrongly, and this fault has now crept into English.

e.g. *Hopefully the doctor will see me tomorrow.*

'Hopefully', since it ends in '-ly' is an adverb, and can only describe the verb 'see'.

i.e. The doctor will see me hopefully tomorrow.
or The doctor will be full of hope when he sees me tomorrow.

But the sentence should be

I hope that the doctor will see me tomorrow.

In Good English we must use the words listed above either carefully to carry their true meaning, or not at all.

Exercise A Improve the following sentences.

1) You say that his crime is not of a serious nature; in that case I will not punish him severely.
2) He was a clever, if somewhat self-centred, young man.
3) She achieved only a low degree of success.
4) Because the ceremony was of an important character, they arrived early.
5) There have been no instances of shop-lifting in this area for over a month.
6) This road surface is in a dangerous condition.
7) The apples he sold were of an inferior quality to those in the shop next door.
8) Hopefully the bus will get us there in time.
9) We shall discuss this issue at our next meeting.
10) In most cases the cars were being driven too fast.

Exercise B Rewrite the following sentences in Good English.

1) The problem is of so complicated a nature that a solution shall be found by no one.
2) The girl is so full of apprehension that hopefully she will be comforted by someone.
3) His injuries were of so serious a character that he was unable to fully recover.
4) If he was not quite in the front rank of Hollywood stars, he was admired by everyone.
5) I don't care what you say, I shall succeed.
6) In some cases the birds were so covered with oil that they died.
7) You are wrong. I saw the animal escape. No one else did.
8) They were reprehended for a crime they had not committed.
9) He was endowed with only a low degree of intelligence.
10) You have been told by the butcher that his meat is of excellent quality; but such is not the case.

Section 8 Phrases to avoid.

Several phrases are used in Journalese which say very little in too many words. These phrases should be avoided in writing Good English. Many of them include the word 'fact'

e.g. 'in fact', 'in point of fact', 'as a matter of fact', 'the fact is', 'the fact of the matter is'.

All these mean nothing more than 'actually' or 'really'.

e.g. *As a matter of fact no one has won the prize.*

means *Actually no one has won the prize.*

Similarly 'owing to he fact that' and 'in spite of the fact that' mean nothing more than 'because' and 'although'.

e.g. *Owing to the fact that he was poor, he could not buy the suit.*

means *Because he was poor he could not buy the suit.*

and *In spite of the fact that he was poor, he bought the suit.*

means *Although he was poor he bought the suit.*

Another bad phrase is 'in any event', or worse still 'in any eventuality'. They should be avoided because they are pompous and because they have an abstract noun.

e.g *In any event we shall come tomorrow.*

would be better as

No matter what happens, we shall come tomorrow.

or simply

We are sure to come tomorrow.

'With reference to', 'in connection with' and 'as regards' are also pompous phrases which should be avoided. All can be replaced by 'regarding'.

e.g. *With reference to your proposal, I have nothing to add.*

can be *Regarding your proposal, I have nothing to add.*

or better still

I have nothing to add to your proposal (or 'to what you propose').

The phrase 'in terms of' is now meaningless, and phrases like 'in the field of' or 'in the area of' are little better. They should be avoided. If you are tempted to use one of them, it is better to think again and express your meaning in a different way. The writer of

How great was the loss in terms of human lives will never be known.

has been tempted by the abstract noun 'loss' into using 'in terms of'. It would be better to write

How many lives were lost (or how many were killed) will never be known.

Other phrases which say little in a lot of words are used in spoken English and are beginning to appear in Journalese. These too should be avoided.

e.g. *'In this day and age'.*

perhaps meant originally

'Nowadays, bearing in mind the state of our civilisation';

but it has come to be used so carelessly that it means nothing more than 'nowadays'.

Thus *In this day and age no one should be unable to read.*

is better as *Nowadays no one should be unable to read.'*

'At this moment in time.'

means much the same, and can be avoided in the same way.'

'At the end of the day'.

perhaps meant originally something like

'At the end of the day's work, when all is done that can be done';

but it generally means no more than

'in the end' or 'finally'.

e.g. *'At the end of the day all will be well.'*

is better as *'In the end all will be well.'*

'Take on board' is a wordy way of saying 'understand'

Thus *He could not take my message on board.*

is better as *He could not understand my message.*

We are inclined to think Americans speak English, but in many ways their language is different from ours. For instance the meaning of an English noun is often expressed by a different one in America. Here are some common English nouns with their American equivalents.

English	American	English	American
Curtains	Drapes	Cupboard	Closet
Braces	Suspenders	Tap	Faucet
Vest	Undershirt	Pavement	Sidewalk
Waistcoat	Vest	Tram	Street-Car
Shop	Store	Autumn	Fall
Biscuits	Crackers	Lift	Elevator
Sweets	Candy	Solicitor	Attorney

Some of the American vocabulary is beginning to come into our own language, but it is doubtful if this is Good English.

What is worse Americans tend to add small words to verbs for no good reason.

e.g *It will be a good party. I don't want to* **miss out on** *it.*

where 'out on' is unnecessary

Similarly *He* **met up with** *his aunt yesterday.*

where 'up with' is unnecessary

But remember that although we use 'meet a person', we use 'meet with' if it is joined to an abstract noun.

e.g. He met *with disaster.*
She met *with abuse.*

'head up' is another fairly new Americanism.

e.g. *A brass band* **headed up** *the procession.*

when we would write

A brass band headed the procession.

or more simply

A brass band led the procession.

A very bad Americanism is 'as of now'.

e.g. **As of now** *nobody may enter this gate.*

We would write

From now on nobody may enter this gate.

We must avoid all these American phrases when we try to write Good English.

Exercise A Rewrite the following in Good English.

1) As a matter of fact he was seen by no one.
2) In any event we shall make no decision today.
3) With reference to your solution of the problem, I agree.
4) I am unable to calculate in terms of overtime worked how much is owed by us to the workmen.
5) In this day and age we must be prepared for any enventuality.
6) At the end of the day the profit made by everyone will be large.
7) I had no expectation of meeting up with a horse on the sidewalk.
8) They were filled with sorrow to miss out on a ceremony of such importance.
9) At this moment in time it is almost a crime that anyone should lack sufficient sustenance.
10) In spite of the fact that we have tried to thoroughtly examine the problem, it is of so obscure a nature that we have had no success.

Section 9 Pictures in the Mind.

A good author sometimes does more than write Good English. He feels so deeply about his subject that his imagination gets to work and creates pictures in his mind. These pictures he must show to his reader. To do this the author must turn them into words that will produce in the reader's mind pictures as vivid as those in his own. So he will not be satisfied with using plain, simple language.

One thing he does is to use the word 'like'.

e.g. *She had very long nails, like claws.*

This produces in the reader's mind a picture of a woman's hand with nails on it as long as the claws of an animal.

Because 'like' means 'similar' we call this device a 'simile'. Similes are not easy to use. Some of them have been used so often that they have become dead.

e.g. *He ran like the wind.*

or, since we can make a simile by using 'as' instead of 'like'

He was as swift as the wind

does not produce in our minds a picture of a strong wind, and means little more than

He ran very fast.

We should not use such dead similes.

Nor should we overdo things and make the simile so unusual that the reader will not believe us.

e.g. *His face was as red as a beetroot.*

although it expresses something impossible, is acceptable. But if we wrote

His face was as red as a ripe strawberry.

no one would believe it.

It is difficult to decide if a simile is too much alive or overdone. If we read

He was a big, strong man, and when he flexed his arms the muscles moved under his skin like little mice.

we might think that was a simile overdone. And yet the idea was first used over 1900 years ago by a Roman doctor when he used the Latin word 'musculus' (= a little mouse) for 'muscle'. But nowadays the word 'muscle' certainly does not call up a picture of a little mouse. The simile that was overdone is completely lost.

Nor when we write prose should our similes be too poetic.

Wordsworth's

The holy time was quiet as a nun
Breathless in adoration

is excellent poetry, but would be bad prose.

It will be seen, therefore, that when we use similes we must be careful. We must avoid dead ones and not strain the reader's belief when we use live ones. Perhaps

The yellow crocuses looked like flames on the ground

is an example of an acceptable simile.

The picture it makes becomes more vivid if, as one poet does, we write

The ground-flame of the crocus.

This does not tell the truth, for the crocus is not really on fire. It is not a flame, nor does it have one. And yet we can accept the phrase because in telling a lie it makes the truth more vivid. This device, which says that one thing is really another thing although it is only like it, is called a 'metaphor'.

In writing Good English we must use metaphors as carefully as we do similes.

Our language is full of words which could show a picture, as if they made a metaphor; but we no longer see the picture in our minds and so the metaphor is 'dead'. For instance the word 'muscle', as mentioned above, no longer produces in our minds the picture of a little mouse. The word 'examine' is derived from a Latin word which means the bar from which a pair of scales are hung. But 'examine' nowadays certainly does not produce in our minds a picture of a pair of scales, and scarely conveys the idea of 'weighing'.

We must avoid 'dead' metaphors.
If we say

She did not grasp my meaning.

we no longer produce a picture of hands gripping something. And if she tries to grasp something so abstract as 'meaning', it would certainly slip through her fingers.

The word 'eager' originally meant 'sharp', but the sentence

He was eager to meet the girl.

conveys no idea of sharpness. The metaphor is dead. We might use one that was more alive by writing

He was burning to meet the girl.

And if we thought that this metaphor has been used too often and so is becoming dead, we might give it more life by writing

He was on fire to meet the girl.

But that might produce too vivid a picture. It might exaggerate his feelings, unless she was a very attractive girl.

As when using similes we must not overdo a metaphor. We must take care not to tell so big a lie that the reader will not believe it. A famous 18th century novelist wrote

I behold the desired port into which I would fain steer, but am
kept off by the foaming billows of a brother's and a sister's envy.

The style of this is a little dated, and we would not now use the words 'behold' and 'fain'. But there is another fault; the reader is not likely to believe that envy is a sea which foams and billows.

If such a metaphor had been used in poetry, it might have been acceptable. We are willing to allow poets to stretch our belief a long way. When Keats writes

Open wide the mind's cage-door,
She'll dart forth and cloudward soar

we think it is good poetry. But we must be careful not to use such bold metaphors in prose.

Careless writers, especially journalists, often use in one sentence two metaphors which do not go together. In other words they mix their metaphors.

e.g. These are the notes which are most consistently struck in the stream of letters now printed in the papers.

Apparently the letter writers are playing the piano in the water.

Here is an example of a good simile written by a famous author.

Here is the fruiterer's, where the dark-green water
melons are heaped upon the counter like cannon-balls.

John Ruskin (1819-1900), The Stones
of Venice.

The picture is clear, although it is little more than a snapshot.

And here is an example of a metaphor used fully and with great effect.

> I am not sensible of any decay of the mental faculties. The original soil has been highly improved by cultivation, but it may be questioned whether some flowers of fancy, some grateful errors, have not been eradicated with the weeds of prejudice.
>
> Edward Gibbon (1737-96) Autobiography.

Exercise A Write sentences containing similes made from the following pairs of words.

1) wave, mountain
2) tooth, saw
3) tear, rain
4) white, snow
5) wind, knife
6) black, pitch
7) sing, angel
8) fly, bird
9) eye, fire
10) fist, hammer

Exercise B Write sentences containing metaphors made from the following pairs of words. e.g. rose, cheek. The roses bloomed on her cheeks.

1) Hammer, fist
2) weave, plot
3) sea, trouble
4) load, grief
5) wind, sweep
6) hope, wreck
7) murder, song
8) wound, abuse
9) blanket, fog
10) hill, fame

Section 10 Examples of Bad English.

Here are some examples of Bad English or Journalese taken, and in some places adapted, from reputable newspapers.

> These changes in international demand for business education, and the implications for increased competition, have not been lost on the business schools. Although a few still refuse to be involved in tailoring courses to companies, many have embraced the idea.

The abstract nouns 'changes', 'demands', 'implications', 'competition' obscure the meaning. The writer would have made his meaning clearer if he had used the corresponding verbs instead. See Section 6.

The metaphor 'tailoring courses' is barely acceptable, and the metaphor 'embraced the idea' is certainly unacceptable. No one can put his arms round so abstract a thing as an idea. See Section 9.

'business education' is not a good phrase, It is quite normal in Good English to put two nouns together so that the first describes the second.

e.g. river bank, picnic basket, sugar bowl

Sometimes we join the two nouns with a hyphen

e.g. pine-needle, sea-weed, water-mill

and sometimes the two nouns become one

e.g. teapot, moleskin, boatman

But the nouns we use in this way are nearly always concrete ones. Two abstract nouns like 'business' and 'education' joined together are cumbersome, and their meaning is not very clear. The above passage might be better written

> Firms in many countries have been asking that the way people are trained for business may be changed. This implies that business schools will have to compete more with one another, and they are aware of this. Although a few still refuse to make their courses fit companies' needs, many have decided to act on this idea.

Here is another example of Journalese:

> On this course delegates with different interests but similar degrees of responsibility were put into groups. One group included a headmaster. In this way the risk of discussion becoming bogged down in detail was vastly reduced. Participants' concerns covered anything from how to develop a more appropriate plan to whether an acquisition should go ahead, and, in the headmaster's case, how to introduce a greater awareness of the financial constraints of running a school, while

> retaining traditional standards.

Here again there are too many abstract nouns; 'interest', 'responsibility', 'risk', 'concern', 'acquisition', 'awareness', 'constraint'. They obscure the meaning.

'Degree' is a word to avoid, and so is 'case'. See Section 7. The word 'case' is used very badly here. Apparently the headmaster has a case, probably a brief-case. The writer begins to tell us that there is something in it, and then disappoints us.

'Discussions bogged down in detail' is an unfortunate mixed metaphor. We might perhaps accept that discussions might go slowly like a man walking across a bog, but it is difficult to see how a bog could be made out of such dry things as 'details'. See Section 9.

This passage might be better written as

> On this course delegates, who were interested in different subjects but were equally responsible for what happened in their organisations, were put into groups. In one group there was a headmaster. In this way members of the groups were not likely to dicuss in so much detail that they made slow progress. They were concerned about many things, from how to develop a plan that was more likely to succeed to deciding whether they should acquire what they had in mind. The headmaster was concerned about making a staff more aware that they must retain the traditional standards of a school without overspending.

Here is a third passage

> The Rabbi did a stint in improverished areas of New York, and this enabled him to hone his populist rhetoric and formulate his unique programme. His first public platform, after a period as a travelling newspaper vendor, was a column for the orthodox Jewish Press.

In this passage there are few abstract nouns to worry us, but 'impoverished', 'populist', 'rhetoric', and 'formulate' are too pompous, while 'stint' is almost too colloquial to go with them. 'Hone' is a vivid way of saying 'sharpen', and it makes us pause for a moment to consider whether such a thing can be done to the abstract noun 'rhetoric'. But in the end we conclude that the metaphor is bold, but acceptable. We are however presented with a mixed metaphor that is too ripe for our taste. The Rabbi is apparently given a platform on which to stand and make a speech; but this platform turns out to be a column, on which he must balance while talking above peoples' heads. Finally we learn that this column is made of paper, which could not bear his weight.

The passage might be better written as

> The Rabbi worked in the poorer quarters of New York, and

this enabled him to make his speeches to the people more cutting, and to shape a programme which was unlike that of any other Rabbi. After a period as a travelling seller of newspapers, he was given his first opportunity to publicise his beliefs in a paper for orthodox Jews called the Jewish Press.

Exercise A. Comment, as above, on the following passages, and rewrite them in good English. In order to do this you may find that you have to use more than one sentence for each passage, The possible meanings of the more obscure words, as given in Chamber's Twentieth Century Dictionary, are printed below.

1) The warning was seen in diplomatic circles as certain to heighten the conviction of the inevitablility of war now gripping the Middle East.
2) Its aims would be the preservation of a stable political balance, the protection of friendly powers, the pre-emption of a hostile hegemony, and the assurance of continued access on reasonable terms to oil resources vital to the western economies.
3) An analysis of the distribution of central support shows a relative shift of resources from the North of England to the South.
4) However the terrorists' bombing campaign continues, and its indiscriminate nature makes it increasingly hard to combat.
5) This system needs the specific resourcing which a registration fee would help to provide, so enabling the employment of dog wardens to enforce the law, including registration itself, and to educate people as to their responsibilities as owners. Such a scheme would be a serious deterrent to the irresponsible owner.
6) His courteous demeanour and undemonstrative appearance made him appear the quintessential gentlemanly product of the Law School which had produced him, but these exterior attributes masked a tough mentality which went hand in hand with dispassionate, almost clinical methods of proceeding.
7) Now we promote small and medium-sized firms; stimulate innovation in industry, whether in products or techniques; foment the creation of companies, and encourage the internationalisation of businesses as a way of improving the image of our country's industry.
8) Trade unionists, still aching from the contraction that pared the economy's traditional mainstays, ship-building and iron and steel, down to profitable size, are eyeing the decreasing employment figures with scepticism.
9) Should ordinary people write books? Those who would answer in the

affirmative have ruled the question elitist, yet it is posed here without pre-emptive antagonism.

10) A television film, which shocked officers who watched it, raised serious questions about the operational effectiveness of a helicopter, which is supposed to provide the backbone of the army's ability to knock out enemy military hardware.

1) **conviction:** act of convincing; strong belief; a proving guilty.
inevitability; state of something which cannot be avoided, or is certain to happen, or is exactly right.

2) **pre-emption:** act of purchasing in preference to others; seizure; act of attacking first to forestall hostile action.
hegemony: leadership; preponderant influence.
resource: source of help; expedient; means of raising money; money; means of support.
economy: administration of the material resources of an individual, community, or country; the state of these resources; a frugal expenditure of money; thrift.

3) **analysis:** a separating of a thing into its component parts; ascertainment of those parts; a table of the results of this.
relative: corresponding; comparative; not absolute; having reference to.

4) **indiscriminate:** not making distinctions.

5) **specific:** belonging to a species; of special origin; precise.
resourcing: is not given in the dictionary as a noun or a verb (see 2).
deterrent: anything that hinders or prevents.

6) **demeanour:** behaviour.
quintessential: most necessary.
attribute: that which is considered as belonging to; that which is inseparable from; a quality.
mentality: mind; mental endowment.
dispassionate: unmoved by feelings; cool; impartial.
clinical: hospital-like; based on observation; unemotional.

7) **innovation:** something introduced as a novelty.
foment: cherish with heat; foster.

8) **pare:** shave off the outer surface; trim; remove by slicing; make smaller slowly.
mainstay: a rope stretching down from the top of the mainmast; chief support.
scepticism: condition of the mind before it has reached a conclusion; doubt.

9) **affirmative:** positive; not negative.
elitist: belonging to a chosen or selected part or group.
antagonism: opposition; hostility.
10) **effectiveness;** ability to produce a result.

Section 11 Examples of Good English.

Here are some examples of Good English taken from a wide range of literature.

> Charles Francis Herries woke when the light of a fine new day was throwing silver shadows across the misty fields. Pushing back the creaking diamond-paned window, standing there in his purple bed-gown he looked down on the courtyard, the thick clustered yews that guarded, as though with fingers on their lips, the house, the ragged stone wall, then, beyond, the river, the thatched roofs of the nearest yeoman's farm, the fields and the dark sombre hills . . .Something told him that at the very last these dark hills would encircle him.
>
> The Herries Chronicle, Hugh Walpole
> (published 1939)

All this is simple and clear. There are no abstract nouns, and every word is derived from the Anglo-Norman part of our language (see Section 5). All the verbs are 'active' (see Section 3). 'Silver' is an unusual way of describing 'shadows'. We might wonder for a moment if it is possible, until we realise that the mist makes them so.

We might also wonder whether 'yews' 'with fingers on their lips' is an overdone metaphor (see Section 9). But as we read on we learn that the man is apprehensive. He is afraid that at the very last the hills will encircle him. That is why they are 'dark' and 'sombre'. So the metaphor is a good one: it calls up in our minds a vivid copy of the picture that is in his.

Here is another example.

> A child is a man in a small letter, yet the best copy of Adam before he tasted Eve, or the Apple; and is happy whose small practice in the world can only write this character. He is Nature's fresh picture newly drawn in oil, which time and much handling dims

and defaces. His soul is yet white paper unscribbled with observations of the world, wherewith at length it becomes a blurred notebook.

Micro-Cosmographie, John Earle (1601-1665)

This too is simple and clear, although some of the words are derived from Latin, and there are some abstract nouns. The metaphors are bold but acceptable.

Here is a third example

> The kingdom of heaven is like unto a grain of mustard seed, which a man took and sowed in his field: which indeed is less than all seeds; but when it is grown, it is greater than the herbs, and becometh a tree, so that the birds of the heaven come and lodge in the branches thereof.

The Bible, St. Matthew 13 (1611)

Nothing could be clearer or simpler than this passage. Every word is of Anglo-Norman origin, and of its 57 words only 10 have more than one syllable. The whole passage is a sustained and effective simile, and we could understand it just as well if we only heard it instead of seeing it in print.

Exercise A Comment, as above, on the following passages, and explain why they are Good English.

1) The dead men looked wonderfully beautiful. The night was shining gently down, softening them into new ivory. Turks were white-skinned on their clothed parts, much whiter than the Arabs; and these soldiers had been very young. Close round them lapped the dark wormwood, now heavy with dew, in which the ends of the moonbeams sparkled like sea-spray.

   Seven Pillars of Wisdom,
   T.E.Lawrence (published 1935)

2) Mr. Harding is a small man, now verging on sixty years, but bearing few of the signs of age; his fair hair is rather grizzled, though not yet grey; his eye is very mild, but clear and bright, though the double glasses which are held swinging from his hand, unless when fixed upon his nose, show that time has told upon his sight.

   The Warden, Anthony Trollope (published 1855)

3) Ransom dropped down on his stomach and drank. Then he lay still to listen and to recover his breath. His eyes were upon the blue water. It was agitated. Circles shuddered and bubbles danced ten yards away from his face.

Suddenly the water heaved and a round, shining, black thing like a cannon-ball came into sight.

Out of the Silent Planet, C.S.Lewis (published 1938)

4) Then Sir Bedivere departed, and went to the sword, and lightly took it up, and went to the water side; and there he bound the girdle about the hilt, and then threw the sword as far into the water as he might; and there came an arm and a hand above the water and met it, and caught it, and so shook it thrice, and then vanished away the hand with the sword in the water.

Morte d'Arthur, Sir Thomas Malory (c. 1470)

5) Now the war has come, bringing with it a new attitude. Youth has turned to gods we of an earlier age knew not, and it is possible to see already the direction in which those who came after us will move. The younger generation, conscious of strength and tumultuous, have done with knocking at the door; they have burst in and seated themselves in our seats.

The Moon and Sixpence, W.Somerset Maugham (published 1919)

6) It was now in the wildness of an angry morning, with a low, hurrying heaven and leaping sea, that showed green under the grey, and rose and slipped away with a roar. The ship was careering with an aching straining crying from every inch of her, aloft and below.

The Bird of Dawning, John Masefield (published 1933)

7) I had more pleasure in strolling about among the old melancholy-looking yew-trees, or the firs, and picking up the red berries, and the fir-apples, which were good for nothing but to look at - or basking in the orangery, till I could almost fancy myself ripening too along with the oranges and the limes in that grateful warmth.

Essays of Elia, Charles Lamb (1775-1834)

8) And the children of Israel went into the midst of the sea upon the dry ground: and the waters were a wall unto them on their right hand and on their left.

The Bible, Exodus 14 (1611)

9) He led the way in under the huge branches of the trees. Old beyond guessing they seemed. Great trailing beards of lichen hung from them, blowing and swaying in the breeze.

The Two Towers, J.R.R.Tolkien (published 1954)

10) The rain tilted a little from the south-west. For the most part it fell

from a grey cloud silently, but now and then the tilt increased, and a kind of sigh passed over the country as the drops lashed the walls, trees, shepherds, and other motionless objects that stood in their slanting career.

The Longest Journey, E.M. Forster (published 1907)

Notes